MW00941357

Pizza,

Weddings,

and

Murder

Papa Pacelli's Pizzeria Series

Book Twenty-Three

By

Patti Benning

Author's Note: On the next page, you'll find out how to access all of my books easily, as well as locate books by best-selling author, Summer Prescott. I'd love to hear your thoughts on my books, the storylines, and anything else that you'd like to comment on – reader feedback is very important to me. Please see the following page for my publisher's contact information. If you'd like to be on her list of "folks to contact" with updates, release and sales notifications, etc…just shoot her an email and let her know. Thanks for reading!

Also…

…if you're looking for more great reads, from me and Summer, check out the Summer Prescott Publishing Book Catalog:

http://summerprescottbooks.com/book-catalog/ for some truly delicious stories.

Contact Info for Summer Prescott Publishing:

Twitter: @summerprescott1

Blog and Book Catalog:
http://summerprescottbooks.com

Email: summer.prescott.cozies@gmail.com

And...look up The Summer Prescott Fan Page and Summer Prescott Publishing Page on Facebook – let's be friends!

To sign up for our fun and exciting newsletter, which will give you opportunities to win prizes and swag, enter contests, and be the first to know about New Releases, click here:
https://forms.aweber.com/form/02/1682036602.htm

TABLE OF CONTENTS

PIZZA, WEDDINGS, AND
MURDER

Papa Pacelli's Pizzeria Series

Book Twenty-Three

CHAPTER ONE

It was only a few weeks before spring, but Eleanora Pacelli wouldn't have guessed it by looking out the window. Northern Maine was still buried in snow, and the forecast wasn't promising a thaw any time soon. Truth be told, she was glad that things wouldn't be warming up for a while. She would rather have a beautiful and snowy winter wedding than one where her guests had to tromp through slush.

"It's just like I remember," her grandmother sighed from the seat beside her. Ann Pacelli had just spent the last four months in Florida and was looking quite good for a woman in her eighties. Ellie didn't think she had ever seen the older woman so *tan*.

"I'm sorry you had to come from sunny beaches to this, Nonna," she said. "Do you want me to turn the heat up? Are you cold?"

"Oh, I'm fine. I've lived here most of my life, you know. Four months out of state hasn't made me soft. I'm glad I get to see the snow, as a matter of fact. I've missed it."

"I think you'll be the only one in town who's glad to see it. I don't remember the last time I was actually warm. At least having a winter wedding means that Russell and I will appreciate our honeymoon more."

"And don't forget your visit in April. I'm so glad you're going to stay for a few days before my lease is up. I've enjoyed my time in Florida, but I've missed you very much."

"I missed you too, Nonna. I'm happy you could come to the wedding. I'm barely working this week, so we'll have plenty of time to spend together before you go back."

They were on their way home to Kittiport, Maine, from the airport in Portland. Ellie was less than a week away from becoming a married woman, and she didn't know whether she was more excited or terrified. This would be her first — and last, if she had her way — marriage, and she wasn't sure what to expect. Would things change between her and Russell? Would they grow closer once he moved into the big Pacelli house with her, or would the stress of living together push them apart? What if he decided at the last minute that he was making a terrible mistake, and she was left standing alone at the altar?

"Ellie, dear, are you okay?"

"I'm fine," she said, reinforcing her words with a small smile. She hoped she hadn't gone noticeably pale. She had been doing that a lot lately. While she loved her fiancé, she had to admit that she was just slightly terrified of the idea of marriage now that it was just a few days away from becoming a reality.

"How is Shannon doing? I'm sure she's excited about the baby. It won't be long now, will it?"

"Just a couple more months," Ellie said. "And yes, she's excited. So am I. I've never been an aunt before."

"This is going to be a wonderful year, I can already tell," her grandmother said. "I can't wait to see what it has in store for us."

Ellie's home was a big, white colonial style house on a curving coastal road just north of the small town of Kittiport. Across the road were a few scraggly trees, and past them was the coast. The property's back yard bordered a state park, which consisted of thousands of acres of trees and trails. It couldn't have been more different from the apartments that Ellie had grown up in Chicago, and it had taken her a while to get used to living surrounded by so much nature and so few people, but now she didn't know if she would be able to bear living in a city with walls all around her instead of nature.

As she pulled into the driveway behind the other cars that were parked there, she looked over at her grandmother's face. It had been months since the older woman had seen the house that she had spent the better part of the last five decades in. She had given Ellie free reign to make any changes that she wanted to the interior while she was gone, but Ellie didn't know how she would feel about those changes once she saw them. That, plus the four guests that had arrived earlier that day, meant that her grandmother's homecoming wouldn't exactly be the relaxing event Ellie had envisioned.

"I'll help you inside, then I'll come back out and get your things," Ellie said. The driveway and the walkway to the front door had been shoveled and salted, but she still didn't want to chance her grandmother slipping on an unexpected icy patch on her way up to the door.

She let the older woman lean on her as they made their way along the path. Nonna looked good for someone her age, and seemed to be in good spirits, but Ellie couldn't help but wonder how much her age was catching up to her. For how much longer would her grandmother be able to retain her relative independence?

Florida is good for her, she thought as they walked up the steps. *All of that sunlight, the warm weather, being surrounded by people who have all of the same limitations that she does... even though I miss her, I'm glad that she signed up for the lease.*

She heard barking coming from inside as she inserted her key into the lock and realized that she had forgotten to call ahead and ask Darlene to put the puppy away. Sawyer was only about four and a half months old, but he weighed enough that he could easily knock the older woman off balance if he jumped up out of excitement — and the young Labrador retriever was almost always excited.

Once the door was unlocked, she turned the knob and slipped through in front of her grandmother, grabbing the black puppy by the collar and pulling him a safe distance away so Nonna could come inside. While her grandmother took off her coat, Ellie clipped a leash onto the puppy's collar. By then, Darlene, Ellie's cousin, had heard the commotion and had come to greet them. Three more women appeared behind her; Ellie's mother, and her two best friends from her previous life in Chicago. They had arrived earlier that morning, and it was still odd to see them here in Kittiport. She had kept her old life almost completely separate from her new one, and this was the first time she had seen either of them in person since she had moved over a year ago.

"Nonna," Darlene said, beaming. "How was your flight? Are you tired? Where are your bags? I can bring them in." Ellie gestured toward the door.

The introductions were simple; Nonna already knew Ellie's mother, Donna, though they hadn't seen each other in years. Ellie introduced her friends, Rachel, who had her black hair cut into a sleek bob, and Katia, whose auburn hair flowed over her shoulders. She still hadn't had much of a chance to reconnect with her friends, but they knew about her grandmother from the emails Ellie sent them and were both politely pleased to meet her.

It took a while for Nonna to get settled in her old room on the ground floor. First, she wanted to meet Sawyer, the new puppy who greeted her with the same happy enthusiasm that he did everyone, and then Ellie pulled the puppy away to give Bunny, her black and white papillon, the chance to greet the older woman without getting trampled by the clumsy puppy.

In the hallway, Nonna stopped by Marlowe's cage to say hello to the parrot. The greenwing macaw had never taken to her as well as she had taken to Ellie, but when she recognized the older woman, she greeted her with a loud "Hi!" — the same greeting she usually reserved for Ellie when she had been gone at work all day.

The tour of the changes could wait for later; Ellie could tell that her grandmother's energy was failing, and Nonna was happy to retire to her room and begin unpacking her things before taking a nap while the other women planned dinner.

That evening, after all six of them had eaten dinner and cleaned up, Ellie retreated to her bedroom. She had lived alone in this house for months and adjusting to so many people being here would take time. Her mother, who hadn't been on good terms with her grandmother for as long as she could remember, had opted to stay in a motel just a few miles away from the Pacelli house. Darlene was sleeping in the same guest bedroom that she had stayed in last time, and Rachel had taken the other small room upstairs that Ellie had been planning on turning into an office before she had taken over her grandfather's study. The study was where Katia was sleeping, on an old camping cot that Ellie had dragged out of the basement. She was grateful to her friends for wanting to stick close and spend time with her while they could, but that didn't change how odd it felt to be sharing the house with so many other women.

As she changed into her sleeping clothes, with Sawyer happily chewing on a toy by the door and Bunny laying on her pillow on the bed, her eyes fell on the wedding dress in the closet. *I'm going to be married*, she thought, wondering why the idea still seemed so odd to her. She'd had months to prepare, but it hadn't seemed real until now, when the wedding was just a few days away. The thought of waking up next to Russell every day for the rest of her life was both terrifying — what if something went wrong? What if they ended up resenting each other? — and exhilarating. As long as the thought of it continued to be more exhilarating than terrifying, she knew she would be okay.

CHAPTER TWO

Besides the fact that Ellie didn't have to drive down to Portland and back, Tuesday was just as busy as the day before had been. *I've spent months planning this thing, how is there still so much to do?* she wondered as she drove back from the community center with Darlene next to her. Her mother was sitting in the back seat, oddly quiet as she gazed out the window. In fact, her mother had been oddly quiet ever since she had arrived the day before. Ellie wasn't sure what to make of it and didn't ask. If her mother had a problem, *she* could bring it up.

"I think we should decorate it on Thursday," Darlene was saying from the passenger seat. "I mean, Friday is going to be busy with so many other last-minute things we have to do, and the place won't be available until late Wednesday evening. We probably won't want to stay up so late, especially not after tonight."

"I hope you and Shannon aren't planning anything *too* crazy for tonight," Ellie said. "Bachelorette parties are all well and good for people in their twenties, but I'm too old to stay up until dawn and drink all night long."

"Don't worry, it won't be anything you won't like," Darlene said. "The evening's about you, after all. It will be fun."

Ellie smiled, but didn't say anything more about it. She hadn't even been planning on having a bachelorette party, but Shannon, her best friend and maid of honor, had insisted. She supposed it would be fun to spend a night out on the town, and not worry about the coming days.

"I think I'll have time to decorate the reception area on Thursday," she said, returning to their original conversation. "Assuming nothing gets delayed, of course. I've got to pick up the flowers and the cake on Friday, and I need to double check the catering menu at the White Pine Kitchen."

"Rachel, Katia, Shannon, and I can handle the decorating," Darlene said. "And your mother, if she wants. We'll just need the key from you. We're your bridesmaids, it's our job to make things easier for you."

"Are you sure? I would feel bad asking you to do anything. You drove all the way from Virginia, and Rachel and Katia came from Chicago. Just the fact that you're here is more than enough."

"I didn't come all the way from Virginia just to sit on my butt and twiddle my thumbs," Darlene pointed out. "We want to help. Starting with the party tonight."

Ellie laughed. "Okay, okay. I suppose it will be nice to have someone else handle these things for once. I don't want to turn into a bridezilla, so I won't micromanage. Just tell me what you need, and I'll make sure you have it."

The rest of the day passed in a blur. Ellie tried to spend some time with her grandmother but got pulled away to take phone calls from guests who were coming from out of state and to approve her cousin's ideas for the reception's decor. Ellie was glad that she and Russell had opted to use the community center for both the ceremony and the reception. It would save them from trying to figure out how to move all of the guests from one building to the next, and no one would have to brave the cold and snow outside until the reception was over.

By the time the sun began to set, talk had shifted from wedding plans to the coming bachelorette party, which Darlene and Shannon had planned by themselves. Neither of the women had given Ellie any hints as to what might be in store for her. She trusted them enough not to worry, and their secrecy made her curious.

"Are you sure you don't want to come, Nonna?" she asked.

"Oh, I'm sure," the older woman said with a chuckle. "I'm already tired, and my bedtime is in about two hours. I would just slow you down. You ladies have fun."

"I don't want you to be left out. I wouldn't even be here if it weren't for you. I would never have met Russell."

"Don't worry about me, Ellie. I want you to go out with your friends and have the perfect evening. If you do that, then I'll be happy."

"If you're sure." Ellie leaned over to give her grandmother a kiss on the cheek, then grabbed her purse and joined her friends by the front door. At Darlene's request, she had dressed casually, in a nice pair of jeans, a sweater with a shirt underneath so she could remove it if she got hot, and a comfortable pair of flats. Earlier that day, she'd had so much to think about that she hadn't really been able to focus on the party that evening, but now that everything else was out of the way, she was excited. She had no doubts that whatever Darlene and Shannon had planned would be fun.

"They're here," Darlene said, peering out the window by the front door and then turning back to the rest of them with a grin. "Let's go."

Darlene opened the front door, then stepped back so that Ellie would be the first one out. Parked alongside the curb in front of the house was a stretch SUV limo. As she stared at it, the back door opened, and Shannon came out. Her friend waved at her with a broad grin on her face, and Ellie grinned back. She hadn't been in a limo since her high school prom. While it might be a bit excessive, it would certainly make the night one to remember.

They started their evening at a tiny restaurant in Benton Harbor — a small town just to the south of Kittiport — that Ellie had driven by a hundred times but had never been in before. Judging from the small, unobtrusive sign on the single door in front, she had expected it to be just another small-town pub but found to her delight that it was anything but. The waiter brought her steak out on a sizzling black rock, and it finished cooking before her eyes. She had to make herself stop eating when she began to feel full, because she knew that there was still more planned for the night ahead of them.

Sure enough, their next stop was a bar where Shannon had reserved a section of tables just for them. Ellie ordered her first drink just as the live band began to play and couldn't help but grin across the table at Shannon. It had been far too long since she had just gone out and had fun, and this was just what she'd needed to take some of the edge off of the stressful days just before her wedding.

"Let's dance," Katia said after a few minutes. "It will be fun. Look, a couple other people are doing it."

"In a second," Ellie said. "You go ahead, I want to talk to my mom."

As her friends traipsed off to enjoy the atmosphere, Ellie turned to her mother, who had been unusually quiet the entire evening. Donna was the sort of person who rarely kept her opinions to herself, so Ellie knew that something serious must be on her mind. A busy bar with a live band might not be the best place to have a conversation, but she wouldn't be able to fully relax and enjoy the evening until she knew what was going on.

"Are you okay?" she asked, moving to a seat closer to her mother.

The other woman just nodded, swirling her drink around in her glass. After a moment, she looked up and sighed. "I'm fine, Ellie. You should be out there enjoying this. It's your evening, after all."

"Look, I know that things haven't always been perfect between us, but if something's wrong, I want to know. Is everything okay back home in Chicago?"

"Everything's fine there."

"Then what is it?"

Her mother put her drink down and reluctantly looked up at her daughter. "You didn't tell me you were inviting your father. If I had known he was coming..." She shook her head. "Well, I would have still come to the wedding, of course. You're my daughter. But I would have liked to be prepared."

"I sent him an invitation a few weeks ago, but I haven't heard back. I don't think he *is* coming. If I knew for sure that he was, I would have told you."

"He left a voicemail on your grandmother's landline." Donna began to fidget with her napkin. "He called while you were out picking her up from the airport. He's coming, and he'll be here Friday."

Ellie gaped at her mother. "Why wouldn't you tell me?"

"I thought you would have listened to it by now," Donna said.

"I never check that answering machine, and Nonna's probably gotten out of the habit of it." Ellie shook her head. "I'm sorry. I had no idea. I invited him because it seemed like the right thing to do at the time, but I didn't really think he would come. He's had plenty of chances to get involved in my life since he left. Why would he choose now?"

"I've never understood why your father makes the choices that he does," her mother said coldly. "This will be the first time I've seen him since he walked out on us. I'm going to do my best to remain civil for your sake, but I'm sure you can understand how hard it will be for me."

"Of course. I'm sorry, Mom. I didn't think. If you want —"

A sharp scream cut her off. The band played a last few, discordant notes before falling silent. Ellie turned to see a small crowd gathered around the door to the women's restroom. Someone else screamed, and then someone shouted, "Help! She's not breathing."

That seemed to break the spell of silence that had fallen over the bar. Ellie got up and hurried toward the bathroom, having no idea what had happened, but hoping she could help in some way. The crowd parted just enough for her to see through the door which someone was propping open. There were two women on the bathroom floor, one laying sprawled on her back, and the other cradling the first one's head, her hands covered in blood.

CHAPTER THREE

Ellie was one of the people who helped keep the crowd back from the scene in the bathroom. She tried not to stare but couldn't keep herself from sneaking glances at the people inside. A woman had come forward, claiming to be a nurse, and was kneeling next to the other two women, searching for a pulse on the injured one. A few people in the crowd had their cell phones out, and she hoped that one of them was calling the police, because she had left her phone in her purse, back on the table.

"What happened?" a man asked, pushing to the front of the crowd. "Is she dead?"

Ellie thought he looked familiar. Was he a customer from the pizzeria? "I don't know," she said. "Did anyone call the police? Do you have a cell phone?"

He did, and he pulled it out to make the call. Ellie breathed a small sigh of relief. At least the authorities would be there soon. She didn't know if the injured woman was still breathing or not, but if she was, then it was obvious that she needed an ambulance. No matter how skilled the nurse was, there was only so much that could be done to save someone's life on a bathroom floor with no medical equipment.

"Ollie? Oh, my goodness, Ollie! What happened?"

A woman with spiky blonde hair came rushing forward, her face pale and her eyes panicked. Ellie managed to catch her by the shoulder before she reached the bathroom.

"That's my sister!" she cried out, her voice rising toward a screech. "Her name's Olive, and it's her birthday. Let me go."

Ellie released her grip, not sure if it was the right thing to do but knowing that she couldn't keep the woman from her sister in what might be the last moments of her life. Everything around her was chaos, and the only thing she could think of was keeping the crowd of people back from the scene in the bathroom, making sure that the woman who was a nurse had the room to work, and that no one tampered with anything that might be evidence. She couldn't see where all of the blood was coming from, but she had a feeling that that much blood couldn't have come from a simple accident. The bathroom was a crime scene.

She didn't know how long it was before a voice with authority commanded the crowd of people to back away from the door. When the first police officer appeared, she felt almost weak with relief. Whatever had happened, it was in their hands now. She didn't know what to do, or how to help, and she was glad that someone who did had arrived.

While the police cleared the way for the paramedics, she rejoined her mother and her friends at the table. They traded wide-eyed looks, but none of them said a word. All of Ellie's concerns about the wedding, and all of the stress of planning it, seemed small now. Someone began to wail, and she caught sight of Olive's spiky haired sister trying to follow the paramedics who were carrying the stretcher out through the front doors. The police stopped her, and one of the officers said something to her that made her calm down slightly.

Then Ellie saw another familiar face, one that she knew much better. Russell was there, making his way through the chaotic room. She raised her hand, waving, and when he saw her his face relaxed. He made a beeline for them and pulled her into a hug.

"I'm glad you're all right," he said.

"How are you here?" she asked. The Benton Harbor police force was even smaller than Kittiport's, and they occasionally joined forces on the larger cases, but she didn't think they would have called Kittiport's sheriff in for something like this.

"Shannon," he said. "She called me as soon as she realized what was going on."

"I thought you might want him here," her friend said. "And I figured it might make things easier. They're probably going to question everyone in the bar, but Russell might be able help get us all out of here before the sun rises."

"Thank you," Ellie said with feeling. She felt better with her fiancé there. He knew how to handle things like this. "I'm sorry. I should have thought to call you myself. Everything just happened so quickly, and then I needed to help keep people from trampling on that poor girl —"

"You have nothing to be sorry for," he said, giving her a quick kiss on the cheek. "Do you have all of your things? All of you? I'll find someone to talk to. They'll ask you some questions, and then we'll be able to leave."

Russell paved the way for them to get out of the bar as quickly as possible. Ellie was still stunned by what had happened, and she knew her friends were too. The limo was waiting for them, parked across the unused spaces at the far end of the parking lot, and it was toward that vehicle that she began to walk. Russell stopped her with a hand on her arm.

"Do you want to ride back with me?" he asked. "I'd like to talk about what happened. I have a feeling it will be hard to get you alone back at the house."

She nodded and told the others to go on without her. She was glad for the time alone with Russell. With all of the business and wedding preparations, she had hardly seen him at all over the past few days.

"Are you okay?" he asked once she was buckled into his truck's passenger seat. "I know you're not hurt, but other than that… it wasn't an easy scene for *me* to look at, and that's my job."

"I'm just in shock," she said. "I keep wondering what happened to her. Then I think of her poor sister, and my heart just aches. It was her birthday."

"The sister's?"

"The victim's. Her name was Olive. Or is, I guess. I don't know if she's still alive."

"The paramedics found a pulse, but it was weak," he told her. "I got a chance to talk to one of the officers who was the first to arrive on the scene while you were being questioned."

"Where was all of the blood from? I didn't see any obvious wounds."

"She had stab wounds in her back," he said. "The woman who found her must have flipped her over to check for a pulse."

"That poor woman," Ellie breathed. "Someone did this to her. Why? Who would commit a murder in a bar bathroom?"

"It could have been a crime of opportunity," he said. "But if someone plotted it out, they didn't do a bad job. There aren't any security cameras in the building, except for one at the register, and the bathrooms aren't in range of the camera. It was a busy night, and people must have been coming and going from the bathroom all evening. No one would have been paying attention to who went in or out. The killer must have hidden in plain sight."

It sometimes made her uncomfortable, how easily Russell could look at things from a criminal's perspective. Here he was, thinking things through and putting the pieces together, while she couldn't stop seeing the blood smeared across bathroom tiles whenever she closed her eyes.

Something occurred to her as Russell turned onto the main road that would take them all the way through Kittiport and back to the Pacelli house. "The killer must have still been in the bar when the woman was found. She couldn't have been in there for long. Do you think whoever it was stuck around until the police got there?"

"It's possible. If the attack happened in the heat of the moment, the perpetrator might have panicked and left right away, but if it had been planned out, or if the attacker was with someone else, they might have stayed so as not to appear suspicious."

She gave a small shiver, wondering if the woman's attacker had been one of the faces in the crowd that she had helped to hold back. Another thought occurred to her. Just how close had she or one of her friends come to being the victim instead?

CHAPTER FOUR

The next morning was Ellie's last shift at Papa Pacelli's pizzeria before her wedding. When she woke up to the blaring alarm, part of her wanted to call in and see if Jacob would be willing to come in and cover for her, but she still had things she wanted to get done before she would feel okay about stepping back for a few days.

For over a year, she had managed the little pizzeria that her grandfather had opened over twenty years ago. Before moving to Kittiport, she had known next to nothing about how to make pizza and had known even less about running a restaurant. She couldn't help but feel proud when she thought about how far both she and the little restaurant had come. Not only was it thriving, but she had opened a second Papa

Pacelli's down in Florida just a few months ago, which was showing more promise than she could have dreamed.

When she walked into her beloved restaurant that morning, her thoughts were still on the grizzly scene from the night before. She hadn't heard anything about the woman since Russell had dropped her off at her house, but she knew that her fiancé would update her as soon as he got news. She hoped that Olive had survived, both for her own sake, and because if she had, then she might be able to name her attacker.

"Hey, Ms. D. How was the party?" Iris, one of her employees, was already in the kitchen, her bright orange hair pulled up into a short ponytail. "Did you have fun?"

"Hi, Iris." Ellie put her purse down and took the time to remove her coat before answering her employee. She didn't really want to go into the attack from the night before but knew there was no way to avoid it without being rudely short to the young woman who had innocently asked how her night had gone. "The first couple of hours were fun, but it took an unexpected turn for the worse." She launched into an explanation of the evening as she tied her hair back, washed her hands, and got ready to cook.

"That's terrible," Iris said, her cheerful demeanor gone. "I'm so sorry. I hope she's okay, and I'm glad everyone you know is all right."

"So am I," Ellie said. "I'm sure the news will have the story soon. If you see anything about it, will you let me know? I have a lot to do today, and I may not get a chance to check online."

"Sure. Do you want me to start taking down chairs out front? I was just about to do that when you came in."

"Go ahead. Did Jacob ask you guys to start coming up with ideas for the specials for the next two weeks? I'd like to look over them before I leave today, so if we need to order anything extra, I can do it tonight."

"The list is on top of the coffee maker," she said. "We didn't put anyone's names by the ideas. We've got a bit of a bet going. Whoever's ideas get chosen won't have to mop up for a week."

Ellie chuckled, pushing thoughts of the attack at the bar the night before out of her mind. It felt good to have something to focus on besides the woman on the bathroom floor.

"I'm glad you're making work fun. I'll let you know soon what the specials will be, so you can call the others and figure out your duties while I'm gone."

The next two specials could wait for now, however. The pizzeria would be opening in just under an hour, and she had work to do if she wanted to get their most popular options ready to go for the customers who just wanted a quick slice and didn't have time to wait for a whole pizza. Since it took the longest to make, she began with that week's special; Alfredo Parmesan chicken pizza with bacon bits sprinkled over the cheese.

She prepared the chicken before doing anything else, carefully cutting the raw meat into chunks before searing them in a buttered pan. One of the things she prided her restaurant on was the fact that they always used fresh food when they could get it. Fresh or frozen, nothing was ever precooked. It meant that some pizzas might take a little bit longer to make, but she thought it was worth it. There were thousands of pizzerias in the world, and quality was the best way to stand out.

While the chicken sizzled away, she washed her hands and began preparing the sauce. Homemade Alfredo sauce was by far superior to anything she had ever found in a store, but it had taken her a while to get used to making it quickly and perfectly every time. Now she added the ingredients without so much as checking a recipe, stirring carefully until the cream cheese, Parmesan cheese, and Asiago had melted into the perfect creamy consistency.

The crust would take the least amount of time to make, so she tackled that last. Thin crust pizzas were the most popular in Maine, so even though she preferred good, old-fashioned Chicago style deep dish pizzas, the dough she took out of the fridge was tailored to make the perfect, crisp thin crust pizza.

After rolling the dough out, she put it in the oven to begin the first stage of cooking while she took out the remainder of ingredients she would need to make the pizza. The onions took only a couple of minutes to chop, and the bacon had been made the day before, and was already cooled and ready to crumble into bits.

It wasn't long before she was spreading the creamy Alfredo sauce over the crust, then adding the chicken and onions, and a generous amount of shredded cheese. The bacon bits she added last, sprinkling enough so that they would add flavor to every bite, but not so many that they overpowered the rest of the flavors with their saltiness.

When the pizza was in the oven, and she had just enough time to throw together a classic cheese and a classic pepperoni pizza before Iris opened the doors and another day at the pizzeria began for real.

I love my job, Ellie thought as she stood at the register, watching her happy customers eating the food that she herself had made fresh just for them. It wasn't the sort of *I love my job* that she told herself when she was driving through the blinding rain to deliver a pizza on the outskirts of town five minutes after closing, but rather a real feeling of joy and peace. *Even if Russell and I were rich, and neither of us ever had to work a day in our lives, I would still want to be here.*

It was a good feeling, one that she had never enjoyed back when she worked a high stress job in Chicago. She knew that part of it was probably due to her upcoming wedding, but she felt unusually cheerful, especially after what had happened the night before. The other woman's attack still weighed heavily at the back of her mind, but it was almost as if her brain had reached a point where all of the stress was just too much, and it had decided to ignore it as best it could.

Since there was a lull in business, she took the opportunity to pull up the email on her phone and look over the honeymoon reservations once more. After a long deliberation, she and Russell had settled on a trip to St. Lucia in the Caribbean. Neither of them had ever been, and Ellie was itching to go to a tropical paradise after the long, cold winter that Kittiport had suffered through. It would be an expensive trip, but between the income from the new restaurant in Florida, and Russell's substantial savings, the two of them would be able to afford it without much of a setback.

She scrolled through the photos of beaches that were white with sand instead of snow, and a turquoise sea that couldn't have had less in common with the stormy grey waters of the Atlantic. It was beautiful and perfect, and just the way to start a new marriage.

The bell over the door rang, and she put her phone away. She may be the boss, but she still had to set a good example, and besides, it would be bad customer service if she was staring at a screen when someone approached the register.

When she looked up, she found herself face to face with the man from the bar. Her good mood came crashing down. It was as if seeing his face had released whatever temporary barrier had been holding the memories at bay while she worked.

"I'd like two slices of your special, and a bottle of water," he said. "Thanks."

He pulled out a credit card, then seemed to recognize her as well. His hand faltered as he reached for the card machine.

"Your order will be right up," Ellie said, not sure what else to say. She didn't know if he wanted to talk about the attack that they had both witnessed the night before, or what she would say if he did.

"Right." He cleared his throat and slid his card, placing it back into his wallet before signing. He hesitated for a moment before speaking again. "Do you know if she lived?"

Ellie shook her head. "Sorry. I don't."

"I hope she did."

Iris brought out the order and handed it to him. He took it, nodded at Ellie, then found an empty table near the door. Ellie was about to slip his receipt into the envelope where they put all of the credit card receipts when she paused. She knew that she had learned the man's name in the past, but she still couldn't remember what it was, and it was bothering her. She found it at the bottom of the receipt and committed it to memory before slipping the paper into the envelope. Wallace Burns. Had he recognized her the night before and come here on purpose to talk, or was it nothing more than a coincidence? She remembered his look of surprise and decided that he hadn't meant to run into her. It was a reminder of just how small their community was, and just how many people had been affected by that night.

CHAPTER FIVE

Ellie's shift ended at five that evening, just before the dinner rush began. She left detailed instructions for the coming weeks and made sure that her employees had every phone number they could conceivably need in case they couldn't reach her while she was gone. She was sure she would stop in at the pizzeria again before leaving on her honeymoon, but just in case something came up and she couldn't, she wanted them to be prepared.

As she drove home, her mind wandered, thoughts of the wedding warring with thoughts of the attack the night before. She had more than enough to worry about without thinking about something that she couldn't control or even do anything about, but she just couldn't get the image of Olive's frantic sister out of her mind. It was easy to gloss over stories of murders and attacks when they were about people she had never met but seeing real grief and fear for a loved one was something she couldn't get out of her head so easily.

She parked as best she could in the crowded driveway, then sat in the car, trying to find the energy to go inside. Even though her mother was staying at a motel, she had been spending most of her time at the Pacelli house, and Ellie felt torn between spending time with her friends, and the woman who had raised her. She liked Rachel and Katia, and appreciated their cheerful encouragement about her wedding, but part of her wanted to try her best to repair her relationship with her mother while she had the chance. Family was more important to her now than ever. She had lost the chance to get to know her grandfather, and she didn't want to risk that happening with anyone else. She knew that if she never made the effort to get close to her mother, she would regret it even more one day.

Her phone buzzed, tearing her away from her thoughts. It was Russell, and she answered gladly, hoping that he had good news.

"Hi," he said. "Can you talk?" Her heart sank at his tone, and her hopes for good news vanished. Whatever he wanted to talk about, it wasn't something she would like.

"I'm just sitting in the car, trying to work up the energy to go into my house," she said. "What's going on?"

"The woman who was attacked yesterday, Olive... she didn't make it. She passed away about an hour ago at the hospital."

"Oh." She fell silent, processing the information, and trying not to imagine how her sister must have taken the news. "I'm so sorry, for both her and her family."

"It's not something that anyone deserves to go through," he said. "I thought you would want to know, though. There's something else I want to get into, but I'd rather do it in person. I was going to invite you over for dinner, but I forgot about your houseguests. Can you get away?"

Ellie glanced toward the house. She rolled down her window and listened. Neither of the dogs were barking.

"I don't think anyone knows I'm here," she said. "I can come over for a quick bite to eat so we can talk, as long as it doesn't take more than an hour or so. They are taking so much time out of their lives for me, and I don't want to seem ungrateful by being gone for too long."

"If you think it will be okay, come on over. I've got a lasagna in the oven, and it should be done by the time you get here."

She was glad to put her car in reverse and turn back towards town. It wasn't that she didn't appreciate what her friends and family members were doing for her, but she knew that everyone inside would want to either go over wedding plans, or pick apart what had happened at the bar, and she didn't want to spend the evening doing either. It was different with Russell — he might actually have some answers about what had happened, which would be better than speculating with her friends.

Russell lived in a small home on the outskirts of town in an old neighborhood that had seen better days. He had lived alone since his first wife had died, other than for his cat, a grey tabby named Sookie who had wormed her way into his home and his heart the year before.

Ellie knocked on his front door and waited for him to open it. She had a key for the house, and could have let herself in, but she had never been comfortable doing so while he was home. That was something that would have to change, since in just a few days they would be living together.

When he opened the door, she was surprised to find the usually tidy house a mess. Boxes were stacked haphazardly everywhere, and the coat closet was open and empty. The couch in the living room had been pushed to the far wall to make a clear path to the bedroom. She had known that he had spent the past week packing and sorting through his possessions to figure out what he wanted to bring with him, what he wanted to put into storage, and what he wanted to leave behind, but it was still a shock to see his house in such a state.

"It's really not as bad as it looks," he said, reading the look on her face. "I have a system."

"Do you need help?" she asked, mentally kicking herself for not having asked before.

"You have enough on your plate," he said. "I'm almost done. All of the small stuff is packed, besides what I need to live for the next few days. Plus, it's not like I need to have everything out of here by Saturday. I just wanted to get a head start on packing. I don't want to have to rush once the house goes on the market."

Impulsively, Ellie stepped forward and wrapped her arms around him. She had spent so much time thinking about how her own life was about to change, that she hadn't stopped to think about everything that Russell was going through. Not only was he getting married for the second time, which must be an emotional experience for him, but he was going to be moving out of the house he had lived in for years and moving in not only with her, but also with her grandmother. To top all of that, he didn't have the same network of support that she did. Besides his brother, James, and his deputy, Liam, he didn't have any close friends.

"Thank you," she said.

"For what?" He sounded puzzled, but pleased.

"For everything. You are the most wonderful person I know."

The oven buzzed, and they pulled apart. Ellie felt better after her unexpected surge of emotion and knew that her worries about their future together were silly. Pre-wedding jitters were something that every bride had, but not every bride had Russell as their fiancé. She had nothing to worry about. No matter what challenges came their way, she knew that they would figure them out together.

They ate on paper plates at the small table nestled in the corner of the kitchen. Sookie rubbed herself against their ankles, and Ellie wondered what the cat thought about all of this upheaval in her life. There would certainly be a period of adjustment for the animals, but they were resilient and would probably adjust more quickly than she and Russell would.

"What was it you wanted to talk about?" she asked as she reached for a second helping of lasagna.

"Just something that's been bothering me about the attack at the bar," her fiancé said. "I might just be being paranoid, which is why I wanted to run it by you before I do anything."

She raised her eyebrows, intrigued. She had helped Russell with a couple of his cases in the past, but rarely had done so directly. Besides, this wasn't his case. The attack had happened in Benton Harbor, and their police would want to handle it.

"What is it?" she asked.

"The murder victim was wearing an outfit that matched yours almost exactly," he said, rising to grab a folder off of the counter. "The lead detective gave me these. I was interested in learning more about what happened, since you were involved. It wasn't until I took a closer look at what she was wearing that I saw it."

Ellie put down her fork and took the folder. She had a feeling that she knew what was inside and was unsurprised to see photos of the crime scene. She was beginning to regret taking that extra helping of lasagna.

Pushing her plate to the side, she focused on the photos, taking note of the woman's clothes like Russell had suggested. She thought back to the night before, remembering what she herself had worn, and was shocked to realize that the similarities in their dress were more than just passing.

The woman in the photographs was wearing a red sweater, blue jeans, and black flats. She even had the same hair color and style as Ellie did. Puzzled, she closed the folder and handed it back to Russell.

"What's going on?" she asked. "What does this mean?"

"I don't know for sure. Like I said, it could be a coincidence. It's a casual bar; a lot of people were wearing jeans, and it's winter, so a sweater is normal. But she would have borne a striking resemblance to you from behind, especially if the killer had been drinking. You know that I've made a number of enemies over the years. It's possible that you were the target, instead of Olive."

Ellie fell silent, turning the thought over and over in her mind. The thought that someone might have died just because they looked like her was horrifying.

CHAPTER SIX

"Come on, Nonna. You missed the bachelorette party. You should come to this."

"Oh, I don't know. I usually just get my hair done. This spa day of yours sounds like quite the experience."

"It's just a manicure and pedicure, a face mask, and some relaxing music. It will be good for you. Besides, I've hardly gotten to spend any time with you since you came back. I want you to come."

Her grandmother relented with a smile. "Okay, if you insist."

It was Thursday, two days before her wedding. Rachel and Katia had planned a spa day for all of them, and afterward, she was on strict orders to go home and relax while her friends set up the reception hall and the room where the ceremony would take place. The next day was the rehearsal and rehearsal dinner… and her father's arrival from out of town.

During the night, Ellie had managed to convince herself that her fiancé was simply overthinking things. She probably hadn't been the true target of the attack; it was too absurd to consider. Yes, it was true that Russell had made enemies over the years, but even if someone out there wanted to kill her to get to him, there was no way he or she could have known where the bachelorette party would be that evening. *She* hadn't even known, and she was the one who the party was for. She didn't know why Olive had been killed, but there was no sense in feeling guilty about the other woman's death when the only thing linking the two of them was a similar outfit. She had a wedding to look forward to. Everything else could wait until after.

The six of them left the house, taking two cars, with Ellie, her mother, Darlene, and Nonna in one, and Rachel and Katia in the other. Shannon would be meeting them there. The salon they were going to was in Kittiport, but Ellie had never been there before. She got her hair cut elsewhere and saw no point in getting a manicure on a regular basis when she had to keep her nails short and neat for work anyway. She had to admit that it was fun to let herself be pampered for the wedding, and she was looking forward to this day even more than she had been looking forward to the party a few nights before.

It was a small salon, so with the reservation that her friends had made for them, it meant they had the place to themselves. As soon as Rachel told the nail technician that greeted them that Ellie was the bride, she was surrounded by people offering congratulations and asking her all sorts of questions about her dress, hairstyle, and makeup plans.

"We want to make sure your nails match your theme," the woman assigned to her said as she sat down. "What were you thinking?"

"Well, it's winter themed, so a lot of white, pearl, and silver colors. The bridesmaids will all be wearing light blue dresses with silver accents. I think I'd like something subtle, though, so no sparkles or anything like that."

"I'll bring out a selection of colors for you," she said, beaming. "It sounds like it will be a beautiful wedding. Your groom is a lucky man."

It felt odd to just relax and soak her feet while someone else did her nails. At first, she chatted with Darlene and Shannon, who were going over the last of their plans for decorating the community center, but eventually, she just put her head back against the chair and closed her eyes, happy to do absolutely nothing for the time being.

"We're going to apply the face masks next," her technician said. "This is a good time to get up and walk around for a couple of minutes if you need to stretch your legs while we prepare the treatment. Just remember, your toenails are still drying, so be careful. There are sandals by each of your chairs, and the bathroom is through the door and to your left."

Rachel, Katia, and Ellie's mother all got up, but Ellie was too comfortable to move herself. She looked across the room to her grandmother and smiled to see how relaxed the older woman looked. This was good for all of them.

She closed her eyes again, feeling sleepy. She heard the bell on the door in the front room ding and sat up straighter as she heard voices rising. Was someone angry that the salon was booked? She thought she heard her mother's voice and sighed. Hopefully Donna wouldn't cause too much trouble. Ellie didn't mind if someone else joined them. There was still an eighth chair open, and the newcomer had just as much a right to enjoy the place as they did.

A few minutes later, after Rachel, Katia, and her mother had trailed back into the room, the technicians returned, each carrying a bowl with a cloth draped over the top. Ellie had never had a face mask applied before, and as the technician uncovered the bowl, she wondered what she was in for.

The cream inside was a bright, toxic green color, and smelled more strongly of chemicals than she had expected. The pamphlet she had picked up on her way into the salon had promised an all-natural facial treatment. She didn't see how something that green could be all natural. Even the technician seemed hesitant. She was looking down at the bowl with a frown on her face.

"This isn't right," she said.

"What do you mean?" Ellie straightened up and looked around. Her mother was already leaning back with her eyes closed, and the mask on her face was a much lighter, pale green — nothing like the almost neon cream in Ellie's bowl.

"It's the wrong color, but I don't see how it could be. We mixed everything as one batch, then separated it out. All the different bowls should be exactly the same. I'm going to bring this to my boss and I'll get you a new bowl."

Puzzled, Ellie leaned back, looking around the room as she did so. Everyone else had their face masks on by now, and they were all the same pale green as the one Ellie had seen them applying to her mother.

The technician returned a moment later, and this time the face cream in the bowl was the same color as everyone else's and smelled like herbs instead of chemicals. Ellie leaned back, still puzzling over what had happened as she closed her eyes and let the technician apply the cream to her face.

By the time everyone's treatment was finished, and their faces had been washed, Ellie felt like a brand-new person. Her nails were perfect — she had chosen a pale, translucent pearly white color with just a tinge of blue. She had reluctantly foregone the gel tips, because she didn't want to worry about keeping up with fake nails during her honeymoon. Her face felt fresh and clean, and ten years younger. She was wedding ready, besides her hair and makeup which would be done Saturday morning.

She waited with the others at the cash register, while her mother — who had insisted on paying — took care of the bill. When she saw the woman who had done her hair, nails, and face walk through with a stack of towels, she peeled off from her group and approached her.

"Did you find out what went wrong with that first batch of face cream?" she asked. "I know the next one was fine, but I'm still curious."

The woman hesitated, glancing over at her boss who was still ringing them up. "We have no idea how it happened," she said, keeping her voice barely above a whisper. "But somehow, green hair dye got mixed in with the face cream. It must have been one of the new girls, playing some sort of practical joke. My boss doesn't want it spread around — business has already been worse than usual this year. I promise, once we figure out who did it, she'll be fired. If it hadn't been caught in time, you might have had to walk down the aisle with a green face."

The technician hurried on her way, leaving Ellie too stunned to say anything as she rejoined her group.

Had someone at the nail salon tried to sabotage her wedding?

CHAPTER SEVEN

After they got back to the house, Rachel, Katia, Darlene, and Ellie's mother took just a few minutes to get changed and grab some coffee before the four of them left again, this time to meet Shannon at the community center where they would set everything up for the wedding on Saturday.

Ellie was glad for the alone time with her grandmother. The two of them sat down in their usual spots at the kitchen table, Ellie with a cup of coffee and Nonna with a mug of tea. A plate of blueberry muffins that the older woman had made fresh that morning sat between them, and Sawyer and Bunny sat near their feet, looking up hopefully as Ellie grabbed a muffin.

"That was lovely," Nonna said. "It was nice of your friends to plan all of that for you."

"It was quite nice, besides the fact that my face almost turned green."

At her grandmother's puzzled look, Ellie dove in to her story about the dye that had been mixed in with the face mask cream. "I didn't make a big deal about it because it was caught in time, but can you imagine walking down the aisle with a green face? I don't know if I could do it. I might have had to postpone the wedding."

"That would have been a disaster," her grandmother said. "Between this and the poor girl that got killed during your bachelorette party, things haven't been going all that smoothly for you, have they?"

Ellie shook her head. "Hopefully nothing else happens before the wedding. I'm stressed enough as it is. I keep alternating between being giddy and excited, and terrified. Is that normal?"

"It is most definitely normal," her grandmother assured her. "You'll be just fine, dear. Russell loves you, and that wouldn't change even if you walked down the aisle with a green face."

She smiled faintly, grateful to her grandmother for her reassurances, but distracted by a thought that had just occurred to her. She had convinced herself that Russell's suspicion about her being the real target of the attack had been nothing more than a fantasy, but what if it hadn't been? The dye in the face cream wasn't the same as a deadly attack, but it could have been another attempt to sabotage their wedding.

Now I'm the one who's being paranoid, she thought, but she excused herself from the table and took her cell phone into the other room, nonetheless. Russell would want to know about this.

Her fiancé answered her call with a cheerful tone, but by the time she finished with her story, she could tell that his good mood was gone. "Walk me through it again," he said. "What happened just before the incident with the face cream?"

"Well, I think someone tried to come in and book an appointment, but it sounded like they were told to leave. I'm not sure that's what happened, but I could hear arguing voices including one that sounded like my mom's voice. I didn't get a chance to ask her about it — she's with the others right now, setting up the reception hall."

"You don't have any idea who it was that came in?"

"No," she said. "I stayed in my chair in the back room the whole time."

"If you can get a description, then I could cross reference it with the witnesses at the bar and see if one of them might be a match. If someone's trying to get to you, I don't want to take any chances."

"I don't want you to worry about me. The nail technician said it was probably just one of the new hires playing a prank. I just thought you would want to know. Besides, how would anyone know where I was? The only people who knew where we were going and when were the people in my bridal party."

Russell was silent for a moment. When he spoke, she thought he sounded hesitant. "Maybe we were looking at this the wrong way. I was assuming that if my theory about you being the real target of the attack was true, then the attacker was trying to get to me through you. But what if it was someone whose sole target was you?" He paused, then reluctantly said, "What if it was someone in your bridal party?"

Ellie laughed, then immediately felt bad about it. Russell was just worried about her. Women weren't the only ones who dealt with stress right before a wedding, and Russell must have been feeling the same as she was. She knew as well as anyone that stress could make people think crazy things.

"I don't think anyone in my bridal party would want to kill me," she said. "I mean, Shannon? Darlene? What could either of them possibly have against me? And I've known Katia and Rachel for years. I used to work with Katia, and Rachel lived in the apartment below me. Why would either of them want to see me dead? I can admit that my mother and I don't have the best relationship, but I seriously doubt she has enough issues with me that she'd try to literally stab me in the back."

"I don't think it's your mother," he said. "And of course, I didn't mean Shannon might be a suspect. But think about it. If the two incidents are connected, then like you said, the women in your bridal party are the only ones who would know where you would be and when."

"They are staying with me in my house," she pointed out. "If one of them did want me dead for some strange reason, then they would have had ample chance to do it."

"If someone's trying to sabotage you without getting caught, it makes more sense to do it in a public place, where strangers would be around to take the blame."

Ellie sighed. "I shouldn't have mentioned anything. I don't want you to worry about me."

"I always worry about you," he said. "Just be careful, okay?"

"I'll keep my eyes open," she promised. "And I'll see *you* tomorrow. Don't forget about the rehearsal."

"How could I?" he asked, laughing. "Trust me when I say this wedding is the only thing I've been thinking about for the past week. I'll be there, and everything will go perfectly — both during the rehearsal and the wedding itself."

Ellie didn't have a chance to think about their conversation again until she was in bed that night. With the wedding just over twenty-four hours away, sleep seemed like an impossible task. As she tossed and turned, she thought about Russell's suspicion. Was he making connections where there weren't any? Normally she trusted his judgment, but she didn't know if either of them had sound judgment about anything this close to their wedding. The fact that his first wife had been murdered didn't help matters either; Russell had always been overly protective of her, and it had certainly gotten more noticeable as their wedding date drew closer. She knew that his protectiveness and concern weren't without cause — she had certainly ended up in dangerous situations in the past.

I don't feel like I'm in danger, she thought. *I trust all of the women who were with me on both days. None of them have a reason to want to see me dead, and none of them have acted less than encouraging about my wedding, besides my mother.* No matter what issues existed between her and Donna, she couldn't imagine her mother as a suspect.

With a sigh, she turned over onto her side, being careful not to disturb Bunny, and gazed at the glowing numbers of the clock on her bedside table. She knew that she was going to be tired tomorrow, but she just couldn't get to sleep. Not only was it her wedding rehearsal, but she was going to have lunch with her father — a man whom she hadn't seen since he had walked out on her and her mother all those years before. What had she been thinking when she had invited him? The truth was, she hadn't expected him to come. She had sent the invitation because it had seemed like the right thing to do at the time, but now she regretted it. She wanted to be surrounded by people who cared about her and Russell, and right now her father was all but a stranger to her. The occasional holiday card couldn't make up for years of absence.

A crashing sound from somewhere else in the house made her sit up straight in bed, yanking her thoughts away from the coming day. Her first thought was of her grandmother. The year before, Nonna had fallen down the basement stairs, and it had only been thanks to Bunny that Ellie had found her in time. If she had fallen again, then she would need help right away.

Ellie jumped out of bed and hurried across the room, yanking open the door and stepping out into the hallway. She didn't pause to turn on the lights as she raced down the stairs, though judging from the glow in the foyer, the lights were already on downstairs.

She skidded to a halt at the bottom of the stairs when she saw that the glow wasn't coming from the hallway light, but rather from the windows that looked out to the front yard and the driveway. Headlights. Someone was parked out front.

Frowning, Ellie padded over to the window and pulled back the curtain just as the lights began to recede. Someone was backing out of the driveway, and it wasn't a vehicle that she recognized. It was difficult to see in the dark, but there was enough moonlight that she could make out some sort of light colored pickup truck, bigger and newer than Russell's. As she watched, it finished backing out of the driveway and sped off along the road away from town.

The sound of broken glass falling onto a hard floor tore her gaze away from the window, and she continued through the house toward the kitchen. The kitchen lights were on, and on the floor, she found not her grandmother, but Rachel, kneeling on the floor as she mopped up champagne and shards of broken glass from a bottle that had been shattered on the floor.

"What happened?" Ellie asked, grabbing a roll of paper towels and getting down on the floor to help her friend.

"I don't know. I had dozed off in the living room and heard the bottle break. I came in here to find it like this."

Puzzled, Ellie looked from the broken bottle of chilled champagne, to the door of the refrigerator, which was shut. There was no way the bottle could have found its way to the floor by itself. Was Rachel lying? Or had someone else been in her house?

She stood up, dumping a wad of sodden paper towels into the garbage bin before making her way to the back door. It was unlocked. Feeling a chill that had nothing to do with the temperature of the air, she flicked on the patio light and opened the door, but the snow was too trampled by the dogs, and she couldn't tell if someone had been out there.

"What is it?" Rachel asked.

"There was someone parked in the driveway when I came downstairs. They pulled away as soon as I opened the curtain and looked out the window." She shook her head. "I don't know what to think. I'm going to make sure everything is locked up, then I'll come and finish cleaning this up. You go to bed."

CHAPTER EIGHT

At breakfast the next morning, Ellie asked if anyone knew what had happened to the champagne, but no one admitted to knowing anything. She hated the fact that she was looking at her friends and family as possible suspects, but either one of them was lying, or someone else had come into the house the night before to do nothing more than break a bottle of champagne and leave.

Why would any of them lie about knocking the bottle over? She wondered. It was a mistake that anyone could have made if they had opened the fridge for a late-night snack. It didn't make sense for any of them to hide it, but it made even less sense to think that someone would have driven all the way out there, found a way in, and then made a beeline to the fridge just to spill a drink.

It was something that she wanted to call Russell about, but she didn't have time to make the call just then. After breakfast, she loaded Sawyer and Bunny into her car along with their food, a crate for the puppy, and their favorite toys, and drove them toward town. The next two days were going to be hectic enough without a puppy underfoot, so finding a pet sitter for the dogs had seemed like the best option. When she and Russell left for their honeymoon next week, the dogs would be going back to the sitter for even longer, so this would be a good practice run.

The new pet sitter was actually a friend of Iris's, a young woman named Cassie who was working toward becoming a vet tech. When Ellie reached her house, it was a simple matter to carry the food, toys, and crate inside and hand the leashes over to Cassie, who both dogs seemed to take to immediately.

"We'll pick them up on Sunday," Ellie said, crouching down to say goodbye to the dogs one last time. "If you need anything, don't hesitate to call. I'm hoping they'll be good for you."

"I'm sure they will be," Cassie said. "I'll take great care of them. You just focus on enjoying your wedding."

Even though she was getting married in less than a day, the wedding was the last thing on her mind as she drove away from Cassie's house. She was supposed to meet her father for an early lunch in less than an hour and could think of nothing but what the meeting would entail. Taking a deep breath, and trying to keep the panic down, she turned into Papa Pacelli's parking lot. She wasn't supposed to work today, but she knew that she would be able to take comfort in the familiar surroundings. It wouldn't hurt to stop in and see how things were going, and it would help to pass the time until the lunch that she was dreading.

The employee entrance opened before she could reach it, and Pete, one of her delivery drivers, came out of the building laden with a pizza bag. He paused to hold the door open for her.

"Hey, Ms. P. We weren't expecting to see you today."

"I had some extra time on my hands," she said. "I thought I'd stop in and say hi. How is everything going?"

"Couldn't be better," he said. "I've got to make these deliveries before they get cold, though."

"Go on," she said. "I wouldn't want to keep the customers waiting."

The door shut behind her, cutting off the cold air from outside. The kitchen was warm, and smelled of dough, melted cheese, and freshly cut peppers. She inhaled deeply, already feeling calmer. The pizzeria was her second home, and it was a good reminder of everything that she had achieved. No matter how the lunch with her father went, it wouldn't change anything. She would still have Russell, the pizzeria, and everything else that made her life worth living.

The kitchen was empty, but not for long. The door that led to the dining area and the register swung open and Rose walked through, doing a double take when she saw Ellie standing by the stove.

"I'm just stopping in because I had some extra time on my hands," the pizzeria owner said. "Pete gave me the same look you did. I'm getting married, that doesn't mean I've vanished off of the face of the earth."

"Sorry," Rose said. "It's just that it's the day before your wedding. I can't imagine coming in to work the day before I get married. I'd be a wreck. There must be so much you have to do."

"Almost everything's taken care of by now. Mostly I'm just trying not to imagine myself tripping while I walk down the aisle."

"I'm sure everything will be perfect. It was so nice of you to invite all of us."

"Well, I wouldn't be where I am today without my employees. You are all vital to the pizzeria's success, and without the pizzeria, I may not have stayed in town long enough to meet Russell." The pizzeria would be opening late Saturday, to give all of her employees time to enjoy the ceremony and the reception before heading to work.

She spent the next twenty minutes helping out where she could in the kitchen, and letting the routine of kneading dough, grating cheese, and making sauce calm her down. When the time came for her to leave and make her way to the Lobster Pot for lunch with her father, she felt marginally more in control.

Ellie took one last look around the kitchen and realized with a pang that this was the last time she would ever be making pizzas as Eleanora Pacelli. The next time she stopped in at the pizzeria, she would be Eleanora Ward.

The Lobster Pot was one of the most popular restaurants in town. It was right next to the marina and had outdoor seating for when the weather was nice. True to its name, it was famous for its locally caught lobster. Evenings were the restaurant's busiest time, but even midday on a Friday the restaurant had enough people inside that for a moment when she first walked in the doors, she panicked, wondering how she would find her father. How much would he have changed over the years?

PATTI BENNING

All she had to go on was the grainy family photo that he had sent her grandmother last Christmas.

Then her eyes landed on a man with greying hair and the beginnings of a goatee who was sitting alone in a booth close to the door. Even though years had passed since she had last seen him in person, she knew in an instant who he was.

Taking a deep breath, Ellie approached the booth. She wavered at the table, waiting for him to look up before she sat down. When he did, she couldn't read the expression in his face. Was he glad to see her? Shocked? Did he feel anything? She couldn't tell. They stared at each other for a long time, then he gestured at the seat across from him.

"Are you going to sit?"

She sat, clutching her purse tightly as she tried to come up with something to say. What did she want her first words to him to be? At last, she settled on

102

something simple, something that wouldn't jump to any of the serious issues too quickly.

"How was your drive?"

"Snowy. There was a storm up near the border last night. The roads cleared once I got down into Maine, though."

Her father lived in Canada, with a wife and children. Ellie had never met any of them even though the children would be her half-siblings.

"I'm glad you made it all right. Where are you staying?"

"A buddy of mine's letting me crash on his couch tonight. I'll be driving back up after the wedding tomorrow."

She nodded. It was probably better if he didn't stay for long. She would do what she could to keep him and her mother separated, but the longer they were both in town, the more likely they would be to run into each other.

They looked at their menus in silence, and Ellie realized for the first time that this must be just as awkward for her father as it was for her. She had so many things that she wanted to ask him but didn't know where to begin.

"Why'd you decide to come to the wedding?" she asked, deciding to start with the most immediate first.

He sighed and put down the menu, fidgeting with the corner of it as he spoke. "I thought I might regret it one day if I didn't. You're only going to get married once, if everything goes well, and that's something a father should be there for."

"You know, I'm having Nonna walk me down the aisle," she said.

It had been difficult to decide between her grandmother and her mother for that task. She owed a lot to both of them, but in the end, she had decided to ask her grandmother. She wouldn't have had the life that she had now in Kittiport if it wasn't for the older woman. She would never have met Russell, would never have taken the job at the pizzeria, and would never have found her place in life. Nonna had been nothing but supportive of every decision she had made, while her mother had never stopped trying to fit Ellie into the path she envisioned her daughter going down, regardless of Ellie's feelings about the matter. For such an important walk, she wanted support, not judgment.

"I assumed you had someone lined up for that. I'm sure she's happy. I just want to watch."

She nodded. That was fine by her. The wedding wasn't about him, anyway; it was about her and Russell.

"I just want you to know that I did want to see you after I left," her father added, unexpectedly. "Donna thought it would be a bad idea. She moved the two of you away to Chicago soon after, then I found out Jess was pregnant, and I knew I had to focus on my new life. I should have tried harder, but I never meant to leave you behind so completely. With every year that passed, it got more and more difficult to imagine what I would say to you when I saw you again, so I kept putting it off. I'm not going to apologize for leaving, because if I hadn't, I wouldn't have been happy like I am now, and I wouldn't have had Justin and Samantha, but I do want to apologize for letting you slip away from me. That was wrong, and I should have tried harder."

Ellie didn't know what to say. Her vision blurred, and she picked up her menu so she could blink back her tears in private. One apology wouldn't fix a lifetime of absence, but she thought it might be a step on the way to repairing their relationship.

CHAPTER NINE

By the time they had finished eating and their leftovers were packed up and ready to go — the Lobster Pot was famous for its large servings — Ellie and her father had managed to find a conversational topic that they could stick to without bringing up the past too much; the pizzeria.

Her father was interested in hearing all about the restaurant's success and was thrilled when she told him about the second pizzeria she had opened in Florida. Papa Pacelli's had been his father's creation, and even though he had never been involved with the restaurant himself, he was fascinated by it. Ellie was happy to talk about the day-to-day running of the pizzeria and what it entailed, and to tell him about some of her adventures in Florida. She was proud of her accomplishments and was glad that she could share how well her life was going with him.

They left the restaurant together and walked down the sidewalk toward the marina where they looked at the *Eleanora*, her grandfather's boat which she and Russell had covered with a heavy canvas tarp before the worst of the snow began. It was odd to think of her father growing up in Kittiport, but of course he had, so walking through town for him was taking a walk through his childhood memories.

"I miss living on the coast," he said as they walked back toward the Lobster Pot, where their cars were parked. "I don't miss the wind and the salt, and that horrible fish smell on hot summer days when the fishing boats are coming in, but I don't think there's anything more beautiful than the ocean. I'm glad your grandmother was able to keep her house. I can't imagine her living anywhere else. She always loved the ocean."

"Do you talk to her much?"

"I call every month or two. I know she's disappointed in me, but even though we don't see eye to eye, she still cares about me. You have no idea how hard it is to come back here."

There was honking down the street behind them, but Ellie didn't turn around. "Did she tell you about —"

Before she could finish her sentence, her father grabbed her by the arm and yanked her to the side, just in time. A large pickup truck swerved onto the sidewalk, right where she had been standing, then tore away, fishtailing down the road as the driver fought for control over the vehicle.

"That was close," Ellie managed to say after a moment, her heart pounding in her chest. "Thank you."

"What was that driver thinking?" he asked angrily. "He can't drive like that in the winter. The roads are icy. He could have killed you."

Ellie looked down the road in the direction that the truck had come. The roads were dry, and they hadn't had more than a sprinkling of snow in the past few days. The truck hadn't slipped on an icy patch; the driver must have been trying to hit her on purpose.

She kept the chilling thought to herself as she said her goodbyes to her father and got into her car, but the instant she was alone, she pulled out her cell phone. She couldn't ignore the coincidences anymore, and she no longer thought Russell was being paranoid. Someone was out to get her.

"I don't have any idea who the truck belongs to," she said for what must have been the third time. After hearing about her most recent near-death experience, Russell had wanted to see her immediately. She was sitting in his kitchen, which looked even more barren than it had before.

"But you're sure it was the same one you saw at your house last night?"

"I'm not *certain* since it was dark out, but I'm pretty sure."

"I don't like this," he said, rising from his chair to begin pacing in the small kitchen. "Ever since the attack in the bar, someone has been targeting you. I'm sure now that Olive wasn't the original target."

Ellie looked down at her hands, which were gripping the edge of the table. She hated that someone had died because of her even if it wasn't her fault.

"I just don't understand who would go to such lengths to try to hurt me. And before you say it, I'm sure that the truck doesn't belong to anyone in the bridal party."

"If it's not someone in your bridal party, then who could it be? No one else would have known that you were going to be at the bar or at the salon at those times."

"Maybe we're getting ahead of ourselves," she said. "It's possible that one of the incidents wasn't related, isn't it? The dye in the face mask could have been a prank from one of the new nail technicians, like the girl who helped me assumed. If the killer is a local, it's possible that they were at the bar without knowing I would be there and decided to take advantage of the coincidence when it occurred. He or she might have nothing to do with the bridal party, or with the wedding at all."

"Then where does that leave us?" Russell asked, looking helpless. "Ellie… I think we should postpone the wedding."

"What? Why?"

"Because if someone is trying to kill you, it's the first place they're going to look. The wedding date and location is public knowledge. They could easily sneak into the ceremony or the reception. I don't want to be a widower for a second time, Ellie. If something happened to you, I wouldn't be able to stand it."

"We can't postpone the wedding. Almost everyone is coming from out of town for this. My dad is here, and I haven't seen him since I was a child. Your parents are driving up, my mother and friends came all the way from Chicago… we can't do something like that at the last second."

"I would happily inconvenience all of them if it meant that you were safe."

"*I* don't want to postpone the wedding, Russell. I want to walk down the aisle tomorrow and marry you. I'm not going to let some criminal with a chip on his shoulder change that."

He sighed and leaned against the counter, running a hand through his hair. "How will we keep you safe?"

She bit her lip, knowing that his concern was real and valid. Nearly being run over by a truck had forced her to admit that. An idea sprang to mind, and she smiled.

"What about Bethany?" she asked. "I can ask one of my bridesmaids to step down — I think Katia is about her size — and she could stand with me at the ceremony and keep close after, like a bodyguard. That way I'll be safe, and if the killer does try something during the wedding, she'll be right there to apprehend them."

Russell fell silent, considering her proposal. Bethany was the younger of his two deputies but had proven herself to be capable in the past. Ellie liked her, and the two of them got along well. It was a fair compromise, and when he nodded slowly, she knew that he would agree.

"Fine," he said. "I'll talk to her, and you give the news to your bridesmaid. Even with her there, I want you to watch your back, okay?"

"I will," she promised. She stood up and kissed him, then grabbed her purse. "I've got to go. We both have a rehearsal to get ready for. Tell Bethany to be there at three, and of course she's invited to dinner afterward."

She felt triumphant as she left his house. Not only was the wedding still on, but they had a plan in place to catch her attacker if he or she struck again. She would never admit it to Russell, but part of her hoped Olive's killer did try something at the reception. What could be better than getting married and solving a case in the same day?

CHAPTER TEN

By the time the rehearsal was over, Ellie was famished and exhausted. She felt bad about asking Katia not to stand as her bridesmaid during the ceremony. All of the bridesmaids' dresses matched in color, though she had let each woman choose whichever style she preferred, so having one woman standing in a dress that didn't match would draw the attacker's eye and might put them on guard. If there hadn't been a need for secrecy, she wouldn't have minded having one bridesmaid with a differently colored dress, but she wanted to flush out the killer if she could.

She knew that she was using herself as bait at her own wedding, and several times she wondered what on earth she was doing. The simple fact was, she wouldn't have a bodyguard forever, and if someone really was after her, she would prefer that they strike when she was expecting it, not when she wasn't.

It was a relief to stop by the pizzeria and pick up the big stack of pizza boxes that her employees had waiting for her. She had debated either getting someone to cater the rehearsal dinner, or going out somewhere, but she figured that pizza would be just fine. They were a pizza family, after all.

She was the last one to arrive home, and she was pleasantly surprised to find that everyone had pitched in. The table was almost finished being set, extra chairs had been brought up from the basement, and the remaining bottle of champagne was waiting on the counter.

"We've all had a long day, and I'm sure we're all tired of people telling us where to stand and what to say, so let's just dig in and have a good time," she said as she put the boxes down on the counter. "We can start being stressed again tomorrow morning."

She would never have admitted it to her friends, who had worked so hard to plan a fun night out for the bachelorette party and a relaxing spa day, but that evening was the best one of the entire week. Everyone she loved was under one roof, and she finally got the chance to forget her concerns for an evening and just relax. She and Russell kept trading smiles, and she was wondering if he was thinking the same thing that she was — that the next time she saw him would be when she was walking down the aisle.

As the meal began to wind down, she joined Shannon in the kitchen to begin consolidating the pizzas. She had gone overboard when she made the order, but it had been on purpose. There would be no time tomorrow morning for a formal breakfast, and she didn't think she would have any appetite once she woke up anyway, but the others might be hungry, and it would be easy for them to grab a slice out of the fridge while they were getting ready.

"You should go back in and join the others," her friend said. "Enjoy the party and let those of us who aren't getting married tomorrow clean up."

"I don't mind helping," Ellie said. "Besides, I haven't had much of a chance to talk to you alone this week. I wanted to thank you for everything you've done."

"Honestly, Darlene has helped a lot," Shannon said. "I think she's trying to make up for crashing on your couch for a month last year."

Ellie laughed. "She doesn't have anything to make up for. I'm glad you have help, though. You've made all of this so much —"

She broke off, a flash of movement by the back window catching her attention. Her eyes took a moment to work out what she was seeing and adjust to the glare of the kitchen lights on the glass. Once they did, she dropped the pizza box she was holding. A man was standing on the other side of the patio door.

Out of the corner of her eye, she saw Shannon turn and clap a hand over her mouth in surprise. The man wasn't looking at them; rather, he seemed to be surveying the back yard. After everything that had happened over the past week, Ellie knew there was only one course of action that she could take. She called for Russell.

He hurried into the kitchen, with Bethany close behind him. He followed her and Shannon's gazes automatically, and Ellie saw him stiffen when he saw the man on the other side of the door. He had turned when she had shouted her fiancé's name and was looking in at them. Ellie couldn't see the expression on his face clearly, thanks to the glare, but she thought he looked just as surprised as they were.

"Be ready to call for backup," Russell muttered to his deputy. "Everyone else, stay back."

Ellie realized that her cry had summoned more than just the sheriff. Everyone else was standing near the door to the dining room, watching with various amounts of curiosity, surprise, and concern as Russell approached the patio door and yanked it open.

Even though Russell had told her to stay back, Ellie couldn't keep herself from edging forward in an attempt to see who the man was. Her fiancé's broad shoulders blocked her view, but at least she could hear the exchange. Even though the kitchen held nearly fifteen people, everyone besides Russell was completely silent.

"My name is Russell Ward. I'm the sheriff. Are you aware that you're trespassing?" he said. "Can you state your name and your reason for being here?"

"Wallace Burns," he said. He told the sheriff his address, then added, "I live just up the street. I was walking my dog, and she slipped her collar. I know I'm trespassing, but I didn't mean anything by it. I just want to find my dog." He held up a leash attached to a dangling buckle collar as proof.

When the man said his name, Ellie felt as if something electric shot through her limbs. Wallace Burns was the man who had been at the bar the night of Olive's death, and he had come to see her in the pizzeria the next day. She wracked her mind, trying to remember if she had seen what vehicle he had been driving that day, but came up with nothing.

She touched Bethany's arm and when the deputy turned toward her, she murmured in her ear. "He was a witness at the bar and I ran into him the day after the attack. He might be the one."

Bethany nodded and moved toward Russell, who was in the middle of checking the man's identification. Before she could get the sheriff's attention, a sharp bark came from outside, and Wallace turned around.

"Teddy!" he called out. "Get over here right now."

A small Shetland sheepdog appeared in the cone of the patio's light, and Wallace grabbed hold of her long enough to slip the collar over her head. He paused to tighten it a notch, then straightened up.

"I'm really sorry," he said. "I didn't mean to disturb anyone. Am I in some sort of trouble?"

Russell sighed. "You're free to go. Just next time, knock on the front door instead of skulking around the back. It looks better."

Wallace nodded. "I understand. Thank you."

He turned and left. Russell shut the door as Bethany began speaking. When she relayed Ellie's information, the sheriff met her eyes as if to confirm it. Ellie nodded. With a muffled curse, Russell hurried through the kitchen toward the front of the house.

"I'm going to follow him," he said. "We have his address, so I can pick him up at his house. I just need my keys and my coat."

"What should we do?" Ellie asked.

"Bethany can stay here with you —"

"No, you shouldn't go alone. I'll lock the doors and keep my phone on me. Will you call me as soon as you know what's going on?"

Russell hesitated, but he was in too much of a hurry to argue. He kissed her, made her promise to be careful, then, with Bethany close behind him, walked into the night.

CHAPTER ELEVEN

It seemed to take an eternity for her cell phone to ring, but in reality, only thirty minutes passed between the time Russell walked out the front door and his call to her. "I just arrested Mr. Burns," he said. "Bethany's securing him in the truck. We're going to drive him down to the station and go from there."

"What happened?" Ellie asked.

"When we got to his house, his truck was parked in the driveway. A tan truck, matching the description you gave me. When I confronted him, he confessed to almost hitting you while you were walking on the sidewalk. Between that and his proximity to the other incidents, it's enough for us to hold him for twenty-four hours. We don't have any evidence yet that he's the one who attacked Olive, or a motive for why he might be after you, but we'll figure all of that out in time."

Ellie breathed a sigh of relief. "You really think it was him? Can I relax?"

"He was nearby every time something happened to you, besides the incident with the dye at the salon which we can't confirm is connected to the other incidents. I do think it's him, Ellie. Don't let your guard down completely, but you can breathe easy for now."

"Thank goodness," she said, feeling as if a weight had been removed from her shoulders. "How long will you be there tonight? You'll still be able to make it to our wedding, won't you?"

"I wouldn't miss it for the world," he said, chuckling. "I'll be there, and in plenty of time to see you walk down the aisle. One more thing. Bethany thinks it's safe if you give the bridesmaid position back to your friend, and I agree. Mr. Burns is in custody, and one of us should be here to question him and deal with his lawyers if they show up. Since Liam and I will be in the wedding, we need her at the sheriff's department."

"Of course. I'll tell Katia. She'll be happy."

Ellie and Russell said their goodbyes. She paused for a moment before hanging up the phone, wanting to say something special, since the next time she saw him would be at the wedding, but she couldn't come up with anything that wouldn't sound cheesy.

She ended the call and rose from the chair she had been seated in. It was time to call everyone together and tell them what had happened — and to tell Katia the good news. Her bridesmaids were back together, and in just over twelve hours she would be a married woman.

The next morning, Ellie woke up before her alarm. Her stomach was filled with butterflies, and not the nice ones she got when Russell kissed her. These butterflies made her want to find the nearest toilet and throw up. *I need to get a hold of myself,* she thought, forcing herself to take slow, deep breaths. *I'm marrying Russell. I love Russell. Why do I feel like I'm about to go skydiving without a parachute?*

A knock sounded at her door, which was the catalyst that dragged her out of bed. She opened the bedroom door to find her mother standing in the hallway, carrying a teacup.

"I know you usually drink coffee, but your grandmother thought that this might help you to calm down if you were feeling nervous."

Ellie took the cup gratefully and inhaled the familiar scent of chamomile tea with honey in it. "Thank you."

"Shannon's here," her mother said. "She said the woman who will be doing your hair and makeup will be arriving at the community center in an hour and a half. You should start getting ready. Is there anything else you need right now?"

"I think I'm good." She hesitated. "Mom… is it normal to feel so nervous?"

"Pre-wedding jitters are perfectly normal. You'll be okay. And Ellie… for what it's worth, I think Russell is a good man. You don't have anything to worry about."

"Thanks." She smiled at the older woman. "I guess I should start getting ready. Is everyone else doing all right?"

"They're busy making a mess of the kitchen and devouring the pizza and the muffins your grandmother made, but everyone's in a good mood and they are all looking forward to today. Before I go back downstairs, is there anything else you need? Are you going to get dressed here or at the community center?"

"The community center," she said. "I don't want to risk anything happening while I'm getting my hair and makeup done, not to mention all of the slush and salt in the parking lot."

"Do you want me to put it in the car? Hand me your shoes, too. I'll get everything ready to go for you."

Ellie was too nervous to do much besides walk around like a zombie while everyone else got ready that morning. She had everything she would need packed up and ready to go and wouldn't be changing out of her comfortable jeans and button-down shirt until it was time to put her wedding gown on. Before she knew it, her mother was herding her into the car where she sat in the passenger seat while they drove to the community center. Then it was just a matter of waiting while Shannon ran inside to make sure Russell wasn't standing around in the hallway. Her friend gave the all clear, and Ellie walked into the building.

She had rented out the entire community center for the wedding, so she had her pick of rooms to set up in. She chose the one with the best lighting, knowing that it would be important for her hairstylist. Waiting was the most difficult part, and she was glad that Shannon and the other bridesmaids were there to keep her company. She didn't talk much but listening to them banter made her feel better.

At long last the stylist arrived and waved everyone else out of the room. She set up her station and Ellie looked at herself in the mirror. She was as pale as the snow outside.

"I'm Annie Mae Johnson, but you can just call me Mae," the woman said. "It's nice to finally meet you. Shannon has told me so much about you. Is this your dress? It's beautiful."

Ellie looked at the dress, which was hanging in its plastic bag in the corner. She felt a moment of panic, wondering what would happen if she had somehow gained ten pounds since trying it on the night before. What if it wouldn't zip up? What would she do?

"Thanks," she managed to say, forcing her attention back to the woman who was about to help her look less like a ghost and more like a vibrant bride. *Slow, deep breaths,* she reminded herself.

"What were you thinking today? I can do anything you want, or if you want suggestions, I can help out there too."

"Suggestions would be good. I know I want the makeup to be subtle and natural, but I'm not sure about the hair. My hair doesn't do much besides just kind of lay there."

"I can show you some tricks if you'd like, that you can use even after today. First, let me pull up some pictures…"

Mae pulled out her phone, then frowned. "I've got a bunch of missed calls from my mother; do you mind if I call her back really quickly? She doesn't usually do this. It might be important."

"Of course," Ellie said.

She was still looking in the mirror, trying to imagine what hairstyle would look good on her, when Mae came back in. She was shocked to see that the other woman was even paler than she was.

"I'm so sorry, but I have to go. My father had an accident, and he's in the hospital. You'll have to find someone else to help you."

Then she was gone, leaving a good portion of her supplies behind in her rush to get out the door. Ellie was left, stunned, for a moment, then rose to go and find Shannon. It was her maid of honor's job to handle emergencies exactly like this.

CHAPTER TWELVE

Without Shannon's help, Ellie might have gone into a complete panic. As it was, she had to force herself to take a mental step back and look at the situation from a perspective other than that of a crazy bride. Mae's father was obviously the more important person just then. Ellie was getting married, and logically she knew that the wedding would go just fine whether she had her hair and makeup professionally done or not. She didn't blame Mae for rushing off to be by his side, but she did spare a few minutes for self-pity. Why was nothing going right this week?

"Okay, we just need to find someone else to do your hair," Shannon said. "Is your mom good at it? I can go find her."

"Katia," Ellie said. "Get her. She worked in a salon back when she was in college. She's good with makeup too."

Shannon rushed off and returned a few minutes later with Katia in tow. "Here you go. I'm going to go find James and make sure everything is on schedule on their end. Feel free to use Mae's supplies — I'll get them back to her later and pay her for whatever you use."

"Thanks for doing this," Ellie said. "I know things have been crazy. You have all been awesome this week."

"Just tell me what to do," her friend said. "Do you want it down? Up? A mix of both?"

"Let's do a mix of both," Ellie said. She turned to face the mirror, watching in the reflection as Katia poked through Mae's things to find the right tools.

"How do you do it?" her friend asked suddenly.

"Do what?" Ellie asked, surprised.

"How do you always end up with everything going your way?"

Ellie burst out laughing, sure that her friend was joking. "Right, because everything always goes perfectly for me. This week has been one disaster or near disaster after the other."

"I'm serious," Katia said, coming up behind her. There was a look in her eyes that made the back of Ellie's neck prickle. "You always got the promotions at work, even before you started dating the boss. You got engaged after six months and were all set to have every woman's dream wedding. Finding out about the affair would have crushed most people, but you just moved and took over an *entire restaurant*, and now you own businesses in two states, you own a boat, and you're getting married to the town's sheriff. How do you do it?"

"I don't own the *Eleanora,* my grandmother still does," Ellie said. She met her friend's eyes in the mirror. "Katia… are you jealous? My life turned upside down when I found out my fiancé was having an affair. I moved to Kittiport and started managing the pizzeria because my grandfather *died.* Yes, I managed to get my life together, but there have been all sorts of struggles between then and now."

Katia didn't seem to be listening to her. "Then I saw you kissing that other guy at the bar, and I just couldn't stand it anymore. You have always had so much and then you just throw it away, first in Chicago and then here."

Ellie's jaw dropped. "I didn't kiss anyone at the bar. I would never do that to Russell. What in the world are you talking about?"

Her friend blinked. "No, you're right. That wasn't you. It was that other girl. She just looked so much like you from the back. I… I thought she was you."

Something clicked in Ellie's brain. "You're the killer?"

Katia stared at her, as if she was just beginning to realize that she had made a major mistake. Then she looked down at her hand, which Ellie saw was grasping a pair of scissors, and her face hardened.

"I thought she was you, and I just snapped. It doesn't matter, anyway. I lost my job just before I came here. You know, the same job we were both working toward for years before you threw it all away like it was nothing. At least in prison, I won't have to worry about finding a way to support myself… and I won't have to deal with people like you who get everything handed to them on a silver platter."

She lunged with the scissors, but Ellie had seen it coming and dove off of her chair in time to avoid the blades. She backed away, putting space between her and Katia while the other woman caught her balance, and grabbed a folding chair from a stack against the wall to use as a shield.

"I can't believe you tried to kill me," she said. She was shocked now, but she was sure the hurt would come later. "The green dye, the broken bottle, the attempted hit and run... that was all you?"

"I thought it would be nice if things didn't always go your way," Katia said with a sneer. "What would your sheriff think when he saw his bride walking down the aisle with a green face? And yeah, that champagne bottle was my fault. I went down to the kitchen looking for something to drink, and when I saw it there, I got so angry. You were so sure we would all want to celebrate with you. As if any of us care about your stupid wedding when we all have our own troubles." She took a step forward, looking from the chair to Ellie as if judging how good of a shield it would make. "I didn't try to run you over, though. That was probably your neighbor, like everyone thinks. I wouldn't be surprised if I wasn't the only person you drove over the edge."

"Katia, I didn't *do* anything," Ellie said. "You didn't have to come to the wedding. I didn't know about the issues you were having with work. I've never done anything to you."

"You never stopped to even give me a second thought," Katia said. "And that is exactly the problem. Nothing has changed. Look at how easily you dropped me as a bridesmaid, then you expected me to just step back into the role as if nothing had changed. That's not how you treat a friend."

Ellie began backing up. The scissors were Katia's only weapon, and they didn't have much range. The other woman followed her slowly but didn't rush forward until she realized that her target was heading for the door.

Just as she started to charge, Ellie threw the chair at her. She didn't pause to see if it hit her but turned to lunge for the door. She let herself out into the hallway and ran toward the room where the ceremony would be taking place, more grateful than ever that she hadn't changed into her dress and heels yet.

She rounded the corner and ran headlong into someone wearing a tuxedo. Looking up, she saw Russell's puzzled face.

"You're not having second thoughts, are you?"

"Katia," she managed to gasp. "She tried to kill me. She's in the hallway."

Just like that, her fiancé was all business and went off to find the killer.

EPILOGUE

"And do you take this man to be your lawfully wedded husband, to love and to cherish, in sickness and in health, for as long as you both shall live?"

"I do," Ellie said. She slid the ring onto Russell's finger, and was glad to see that it was a perfect fit, and a perfect match for her own.

"Eleanora and Russell, having witnessed your vows to one another, it is my joy to present you to all gathered here as husband and wife." Turning to Russell, he said, "You may kiss the bride."

After the rush of people cleared, most of them heading toward the reception hall just a few rooms away, Ellie and Russell got the first chance to be alone together that they had had since the events earlier that morning. She walked with him down the hall that led to the dressing room where her more comfortable shoes were waiting for her. She paused long enough to wave to her father, who beamed and gave her a thumbs up before slipping out through the front doors. He might have been able to brave seeing her for the first time in years, but he was still adamant about avoiding her mother. She had the feeling that he might visit again soon, and she was willing to take the time to begin getting to know him again. He was far from perfect, but he was still her father, and she thought that it was time to let some grudges go.

"I don't understand," she said as she and Russell resumed walking. "Were she and Wallace both trying to kill me?"

"We'll know more when I get back to the sheriff's department this evening — ah, tomorrow, I mean," he said, correcting himself with a grin. "Don't worry,

I won't leave you alone on our wedding night. But considering what Katia said to you, I think it's likely that Mr. Burns was telling the truth. The night he was in your driveway, he was just using it to turn around because he had forgotten his wallet at home. The day he almost hit you, he claims he was reading a text message on his cell phone and drove off the road accidentally. He told me he didn't even know he had almost hit somebody, and he seemed to be glad that you were okay."

"That's good, I suppose," she said. "I think one person trying to kill me at a time is more than enough. I just can't wrap my mind around how much she resented me." She shook her head.

"Hey, it's our wedding day. Save the unhappy thoughts for another time." He stopped walking and turned her toward him, kissing her more deeply than he had during the ceremony. "We've only got one wedding day, so let's make the most of it."

"I can agree to that," she said. She grinned, the full impact of the ceremony hitting her for the first time. "Russell, we're *married.*"

"I know." He grinned back at her. "I was there. And I hear that there's going to be an amazing reception starting in just a few minutes. Let's go and have fun. We can save everything else for another day."

Ellie couldn't argue with that, and she didn't want to. With her husband by her side, nothing could dampen her mood. Her wedding day might not have gone exactly as planned, but in this moment, it was perfect.

Made in the USA
Middletown, DE
23 February 2023